THE ZEBRA

Text © 1993 Hiawyn Oram. Illustrations © 1993 by David McKee. All rights reserved. Printed in Great Britain.
First published in 1992 by Andersen Press Ltd., 20 Vauxhall Bridge Road, London SW1V 2SA. First U.S. edition
published in 1993 by Hyperion Books for Children, 114 Fifth Avenue, New York, New York 10011.

1 3 5 7 9 10 8 6 4 2

This book is set in 13 pt. Palatino roman.
The art is created with pastel and watercolor paintings.

Oram, Hiawyn.
    Out of the blue: poems about color/written by Hiawyn Oram:
illustrated by David McKee—1st U.S. ed.
        p. cm.
    "First published in 1992 by Andersen Press . . . London"—T.p.
verso.
    Summary: A collection of poems and verses all about color,
including "Red Tape," "Scared Yellow," "Gray Heads," and "The Green-eyed Monster."
    ISBN 1–56282–469–4 (trade)—ISBN 1–56282–470–8 (lib. bdg.)
    1. Color—Juvenile poetry. 2. Children's poetry, English.
[1. Color—Poetry. 2. English poetry.]   I. McKee, David, ill.
    II. Title.
    PR6065.R28093   1993
    821'.914—dc20   92-55044
                                                            CIP
                                                            AC

OUT of the BLUE

Poems About Color

WRITTEN BY

HIAWYN ORAM

ILLUSTRATED BY

DAVID McKEE

HYPERION BOOKS FOR CHILDREN

NEW YORK

Red Rags to Little Bull

Little Bull's mother was crying
   "Oh, I knew it would happen, I knew,
You are next on the list for the bullrings
   And soon you'll be dead in one, too."
Now, Little Bull just adored living
   And an end to it sounded too grim
So he asked for a good explanation
   Why bullrings meant curtains for him.
"Red rags, my dear, red," wept his mother
   "Though, the Lord knows, it doesn't make sense
They will taunt you with red till you charge them
   Then kill you in mock self-defense."
"Won't charge then," said Little Bull staunchly
   "I'll ignore them, avoid being dead."
"You will charge," said his mother most glumly
   "Bulls cannot resist charging red."
Well, they took him away to the bullrings
   As he went he said, "Mother, no tears
You will find I'll be back" – and he was, too,
   Relieving her worst dreads and fears.
"A miracle this!" she cried, "Tell me
   How it happened, brave son, you're not dead?"
"I just closed my eyes tight," he smiled wisely,
   "I wouldn't and now won't see red!"
But famous last words from a bull, for
   In the summer the fields were all full
With a million innocent poppies
   Being charged by Little Bull.

Red Skies

Red sky at night
Is a shepherd's delight
Red sky in the morning
Is a shepherd's warning

Two Redheads Are Better Than One

Rachel the Redhead was all in despair
    Hating the sight of her head of red hair
She lived in the bathroom but couldn't repair
    Not the flaming red red of THAT head of red hair

Then along came a knight in some armor all shining
    Who said to her, "Rachel, now why are you whining?
I've searched the whole earth for a head to compare
    With the flaming red red of MY head of red hair."

Then he took off his helmet, how Rachel did stare
    Seeing the sight of his head of red hair
And soon they were married and loving the glare
    Of the flaming red red of TWO heads of red hair

Red Berries

Nature's no fool, though she went to no school
Makes berries turn red when it's time they spread
So that birds, in their greed, will carry the seed

Red Tape

A stickler from down in the Cape
Liked everything tied in red tape
But what a to-do
When he found *he* was too
And no one would help him escape

The Cardinal's Hat

The cardinal stood in his ruby red hat
    Looking longingly up at the sky
"I love God so much and I'm sure He can't know"
    He said with a deep reverend sigh
"Then go there at once and tell him yourself,"
    Sang a plain little bird passing by
"But how?" said the cardinal. "I have no wings
    And without them I doubt I could fly"
"Then I shall go for you," the little bird sang
    "But give me your ruby red hat
For it's hard to get in to the houses of God
    And I certainly won't without that."
So the cardinal gave him his hat, the poor fool
    And, laughing, the bird flew away
And quite unappalled by the trick — he's been called
    A cardinal bird to this day.

Red Herring

There once was a pack of foxhounds
    Being trained to follow a scent
Red herrings were dragged through the bushes
    And off the obedient went
Except for the smartest hound dog
    Who refused with a sniff and a sneer,
"It is fox that a foxhound should follow
    And that's herring—I can smell it from here."
And from that day to this, a red herring's
    An expression by which it is meant
That someone is trying to coax you
    To follow a falsely laid scent.

Red Breast

Said Swallow to the Robin,
  "It really gets me down
That you have such a red
  breast while mine is mainly
  brown"
Said Robin, "You migrate, sir,
  and so you do not know
A robin's breast is red, sir, to
  brighten up the snow."

Red Giants and Red Dwarfs

The stars are suns, giants, and dwarfs
   And it's fun to recognize
That each is very different
   In character and size
The youngest ones are hottest
   The heat is white they shed
It's older suns that simmer down
   And quietly glower red

Song of the Carnivore

Oh, I do like lobster, *sang the Carnivore*
   And I will wear cherry, which I quite adore
And I have a pair of shoes in the vein of cheese
   And a hat in the color of strawberries
And I will say currant's very bright and bold
   While a flame red chili doesn't leave me cold
But talk of a red good enough to eat
   And there's NOTHING like the BLOOD-RED RED OF MEAT!

Embarrassment

You might wish it was white, you might wish it was blue
   You might wish that it never would happen to you
But scarlet, tomato, crimson, or rose
   Is the way that it happens, the way that it goes
When you're put on the spot or they call out your name
   Or your mother is making you curl up with shame
You can feel it all fiery and rising apace
   Right up from your shoe caps full speed to your face
You can wish it was primrose or deep bottle green
   Or something less glaring and easily seen
But there is no escaping, it has to be said –
   Embarrassment ALWAYS comes in red

Sunny Reflections

Without the sun we wouldn't have life
    We wouldn't have wheat, we wouldn't have corn
Without the sun we wouldn't have known
    We didn't have life—we wouldn't be born

Ripe Corn

Her hair was the color of ripened corn
A color, she thought, she couldn't adorn
Till binding it up with cornflowers blue
The mouse said, "Cor!" and the cows said, "Moo"
And the farmer's son said, "I love you!"

Dandelion

The dandelion though but a weed
Like golden cheer does grow
And when its flower has turned to puff
It kindly lets us know
"He loves me, he loves me not, he loves me,
    I KNEW IT!
He loves me, he loves me not—oh,
    Dandelion, YOU BLEW IT!"

Straw's Gold

Though straw looks gold, to most of us
It is a simple thing
To those with wintering cows to feed
Straw is king.

The Sunflower and the Crocus

Said the Sunflower to the Crocus,
"For man's nutritional needs
I'm most important—I give my seeds."

Said the Crocus to the Sunflower,
"Your seeds are good, of course,
But I give them saffron—I flavor sauce."

Yellow Dog Running

The dog was a dirty yellow
   His legs were crippled and thin
His life was the life of an outcast
   There was no one who'd take him in
The kids thought it most amusing
   When Sam suggested some fun
And picked up a stone and threw it
   Crying, "Let's make Yellow Dog run!"
But stranger than any fiction
   Sam suddenly fell on hard times
And one of his legs was left crippled
   By one of his hit-and-run crimes
And now when a kid goes crying,
   "Let's go make Yellow Dog run!"
The answer comes back from the others:
   "Yeah, sure – but say – which one?"

Scared Yellow

There once was a cowardly fellow
Who wobbled, when challenged, like jello
   Though his hair hadn't grayed
   From being afraid
His skin had gone cadmium yellow

The Primrose Path

I took the primrose path through woods
When I was six or seven
And thought I must have stumbled on
The scenic route to heaven

Song of the Lemon

Sour as puss, and bitter maybe
   But think of me sliced in hot black tea
And what of the scent of Lemon Verbena
   When added to soap—you'll never feel cleaner
And who put the lemon in lemon meringue
   Or gave bags of sherbet their twist and their tang
And some time ago when sailors grew nervy
   And crabby and scabby, I cured them of scurvy
So no matter how bitter my rind or my juices
   The song that I sing is – a lemon has uses

Variations on a Yellow Theme

Cowardy cowardy custard,
Can't eat bread and mustard

Cowardy cowardy custard
Three bags of mustard
One for you
And one for me
And one for cowardy custard

Cowardy cowardy custard
Your bones will turn to mustard

Cowardy cowardy custard
Dip your head in Granny's mustard

Cowardy cowardy custard
Fell in his mother's mustard
The mustard was hot
He swallowed the lot
Cowardy cowardy custard

Yellow with Age

See how old paper withers and looks
    Ancient old photographs, dusty old books
Watch how old leaves, linen, and skin
    Alter to mirror the changes within
Mark how with age things gradually mellow
    React to the air and oxidize yellow

Yellow Soap

To make a bar of yellow soap
And wash yourself of odor
Mix some tallow with some rosin
And a spoon of soda

Night

Black as night, they say, for black is night
    The velvet of her cloak absorbs all light
She gives no quarter and she asks for none
    And neither pines nor hankers for the missing sun
Black as jet, she strides, black pearl is night
    Who gives her loyal subjects undimmed sight
The owl, the bat, the sweet-songed nightingale
    To all who live and walk with her she lifts her veil
Till they become the jewels that glitter in her crown
    And wish their Queen's ascendance and the sun forever down

Mourning Dress

They all wore black to Grandpa's funeral
    It seemed a way to say,
"The color that you brought our lives
    Has dimmed and gone away"
Then, in a week, to our surprise
    Gran started wearing red
But she explained, "I'll live for two
    Now one of us is dead"

Licorice Sticks

Some say "comforters" and some say "chews"
    And some say "lollies-on-sticks"
But I say, "Half-a-pound-of-allsorts-please
    An'-sixteen-stickerish-licks"

The Black Hole

Somewhere in the galaxy it happened
A massive star collapsed like shattered glass
Till gravitation pulled the bits together
So densely not a ray of light could pass
Then round itself—this tightly shrunken
    matter
This dark and suicidal shrunken shape—
It gathered a protectorate, it colonized the
    space
Making sure from this protectorate not a thing
    could now escape…
Then a chorus of the mothers of young
    meteors and 'ites
The planets and the comets and the smaller
    cluster lights
Rose like any chorusing of frightened mothers
    might:
DON'T GO NEAR THE BLACK HOLE,
DON'T GO NEAR THE BLACK HOLE,
DON'T GO NEAR THE BLACK HOLE,
    LITTLE DARLINGS, TONIGHT!

The Crow, the Raven, and the Rook

The Crow, the Raven, and the Rook
    All met to have a jaw
'Bout history and politics
    And why they weren't loathed more
"I cheat, I swindle, and I thieve
    I have a raucous caw,"
Declared the Rook. "I'm quite perplexed
    That I'm not loathed much more."
"I feed on carrion and on flesh
    The rotting I adore,"
The Raven said. "I'm quite perplexed
    That I'm not loathed much more."
"I go unchecked, I steal their grain,
    I eat their chickens raw,"
Announced the Crow. "I'm most surprised
    We're ALL not loathed much more—
Yet feel that for the reason
    We needn't search too far
It's simply that they understand
    What characters we are."

Joseph Addison's Ode

Blackbirds in the garden
Eating up the cherries
Frankly for their cheerful songs
I'd give them all the berries

The Black Patch

My uncle wears a black patch when he comes
   to us for tea
And he says he was a pirate, which I'm sure he
   says for me
'Cause though he knows of pirate gold he'll dig
   up one dark night—
SOME days it's his left eye that he patches—
   some the right

Black Book

"You're going down in my Black Book
  You haven't passed the test,"
The King cried to his Admiralty.
  "Your crimes you've not confessed."
"Oh please not that, Your Majesty
  Not down with all the rest."
The Admiral wept upon his knees,
  "We did our level best."
"Then best just wasn't good enough
  I'll hear no more of it
You've fallen out of favor,"
  Yelled the King, "AND IT IS WRIT!"

Blackbirds

Sing a song of sixpence
  A pocket full of rye
Four and twenty blackbirds
  Baked in a pie
When the pie was opened
  The birds began to sing
Wasn't that a dainty dish
  To set before a king?

The King was in his countinghouse
  Counting out his money
The Queen was in her parlor
  Eating bread and honey
The maid was in the garden
  Hanging out the clothes
When down flew a blackbird
  And pecked off her nose

Little Boy Blue

Little Boy Blue, come blow your horn
    The sheep's in the meadow, the cow's in the corn
Where is the boy who looks after the sheep?
    He's under the haystack fast asleep
Will you awake him? No, not I
    For if I do he will only cry

The Bushman's Bluey

Over his shoulder the Bushman slings
    All that he owns, important things
A can for his billy, a hunting knife
    And p'rhaps if he had one, one good wife
And he bundles them up in a blanket of blue
    And wherever he goes, that Bluey goes, too

Out of the Blue

Out of the blue, into the blue
The meteor spun and spun
Toward the blue of infinity
From the blue where it all began

Blue-eyed Boy
A Confusing Story

Our brother Jack was favorite
  Ma bought him every toy
She used to stroke his hair and say,
  "And how's my blue-eyed boy?"
Well, we could hardly bear that
  It made us feel so down
For Jess and I had blue eyes
  And Jack's were walnut brown.

Blue Blood

When we're cold our hands go blue
   As if our blood had gone blue, too,
Just like they say of Queens and Kings
   And Duchesses and Counts and things
Which seems to show quite possibly
   To some extent or small degree
We're all quite royal and not been told
   And only show it when we're cold

The Ballad of Blue-Stocking Bella

Blue-Stocking Bella was clever as clever
   Blue-Stocking Bel was a swat
Her head she kept down
   In her books with a frown
She was crazy to know what was what

Blue-Stocking Bella was clever as clever
   Blue-Stocking Bel was a brain
When teased and called "Smarty"
   She took up karate
And never got laughed at again

Neverness

Once in a blue moon, they say
Once in a blue moon
But as the moon is never blue
You know it won't be soon

Ballad of Blue China

There's a joy without canker or cark
There's a pleasure eternally new
'Tis to gloat on the glaze and the mark
Of china that's ancient and blue

Forget-Me-Nots

Forget-Me-Not, Forget-Me-Not
Though your flower is small
Forget me not, Forget-Me-Nots
And I'll remember all

The Blues

A bluebottle's blue
    And a bluebell's blue
And so is a cloudless sky
    And the eggs of a coot
And a sailor's suit
    And a helping of blueberry pie

An eye can be blue
    And a bruise can be, too
But surely no blue can compare
    To the one that is found
When we're flailing around
    In the bottomless depths of despair

Carpet of Blue

It can happen, it can happen
　　Late in April, early May
You don't think you'll come across it
　　So it takes your breath away
You'll have entered on the hillside
　　Through the fence you always use
To the woods you always walk in
　　Round the way you always choose
When you stumble on the bluebells
　　And it seems a fact to you
That there's never been a carpet
　　Quite so beautiful or blue

Blue Jeans

Now, everyone has at least one favorite pair
　　For days when the question is "What shall I wear?"
But Barnaby Brown, though we tease him and scoff
　　He lives in his favorites and won't take them off
He wears them on weekends, he wears them to school
　　He wears them to bed and to bath, as a rule
His mother now says (though she used to make scenes)
　　That Barnaby thinks he was BORN in blue jeans

The Devil and the Deep Blue Sea

The boy walked down the tongue of rock that ran into the sea
　　While knowing well it was no place for any boy to be
But in his heart there was a need, a deep and desperate wish
　　To match the other boastful boys who went down there to fish
So leaning from the treach'rous edge he cast what bait he'd got
　　And waited till he felt he had a lobster in each pot
But as he bent to draw them up, a chill ran down his spine
　　As from behind a laugh rang out, "And now, my boy, you're mine!"
He turned and dropped his precious pots in horror and in shock
　　The Devil was advancing, nimble-footed, down the rock!

"What do you want?" his voice was shrill, a challenge and a plea
   The Devil answered grinning, "That you do some work for me…
And as you're in my clutches and there's nowhere else to go
   I hope you'll not be stupid and consider saying no…"
The boy looked round in panic for a possible escape
   But caught between two evils he was in a dreadful scrape
In front the Devil blocked the way, behind him lay the sea
   So deep and blue and fathomless. Both graves, he thought, for me.
But then a bobbing lobster pot by chance just caught his eye
   He jumped and clung on for his life, till land at last was nigh
And once ashore the boy made vows to fish contentedly
   And nevermore be caught between the devil and blue sea.

Wearing the Pink

Maybe they're color-blind, maybe it's worse
Maybe the hunters of fox are perverse
Which could be embarrassing if you'd not heard
And arrived for the hunt having trusted their word
For, as if to confuse us and make our hearts sink
They go about calling their red jackets pink
And then—there's no end to these verbal high jinks—
While wearing red jackets they call themselves "pinks!"

Little Pink Pigs

Little pink pigs with your curly tails
No wonder the noise you're makin'
For today you're the farmyard darlin' dears
And tomorrow you're ham and bacon!

Coral Trout

Down in the ocean the Coral Trout is swimming
The Coral Trout is grazing but she doesn't come to grief
For down in the ocean the Coral Trout looks coral
And her predators can't tell her from a coral Coral Reef

Shocking Pink

Shocking pink is shocking
And it never shows restraint
And in garters round a stocking
It can cause strong men to faint

Pink Blancmange

Wibbly wobbly pink blancmange
Served with lumpy custard
I would rather eat my shoe
Served with English mustard

Newborn Pink

Pink from your top
 Pink to your toes
Wrapped in warm blankets
 And soft baby clothes
That you're so newborn
 Quite clearly shows
In the pink from your top
 To your little pink toes

In the Pink

To be in the pink is to be in the prime
 And the peak of a perfect condition
With each muscle so fit you'll be entering it
 In a Picture-of-Health competition
To be in the pink is to feel like a cloud
 Of pinks—and as fit as a fiddle
With a fresh glowing skin you're quite comfortable in—
 And NO saggy bits in the middle

Smoke

The gray smoke rising from the valley
In a thin but strong and steady winding line
When you're trudging through a cold and rainy evening
Somehow comes as such a very welcome sign
For if there's smoke, then somewhere in the valley,
A fire must burn that gives a warming glow
A kettle's on the boil, people live there that's for sure
Which is always very comforting to know

Rooftops in the Rain

On any dry and cloudless day
It's true to say that slate looks gray
But when the roofs are wet with rain
Before you say it, look again

Dapple Gray

I took my horse to market
And lost her on the way
For dappled were the moors with rain
And she was dapple gray

Fog, Filthy Air & Graymalkin

First Witch
When shall we three meet again?
In thunder, lightning, or in rain?
Second Witch
When the hurlyburly's done
When the battle's lost and won.
Third Witch
That will be ere the set of sun.
First Witch
Where the place?
Second Witch
Upon the heath.
Third Witch
There to meet with Macbeth.
                    (a cat miaows from off)
First Witch
I come, Graymalkin!
                    (a toad croaks from off)
Second Witch
Paddock calls.
Third Witch
Anon!
All Three Witches
Fair is foul, and foul is fair:
Hover through the fog and filthy air.

The Gray Friar

A Friar from Gray Friar's Friary
Was found with a blasphemous diary
It said, "Oh dear God
Please don't find this odd
But I long for a habit more fiery"

Gray Wolf

Why do you howl so, Great Gray Wolf
And silence sabotage
Is it because the Moon's so bright
It spoils your camouflage?

Gray Heads

Is it with too much worrying
  That grown-ups' heads go gray
From endless making unmade beds
  And slaving hard all day?
Is it from too much stress and strife
  And not going out to play?
Or all their wayward children
  Who have made them go that way?
Well, maybe gray is hurried on
  By these and other scenes
But mostly there's no helping it
  It's programmed in the genes

Gray Dove and the Graybeard

Old Graybeard had a gray beard
  And sat upon the wall
And sat there quite unhearing
  Till came the Gray Dove's call,
"Oh, Graybeard, lend me nesting
  Inside your stately beard
Then I shall pass unnoticed
  And all my brood be reared."

Song of the Gray Suits

Gray, gray, gray
  Day after day after day
If you want to do well in the Dull Brigade
  You mustn't be seen in another shade
But gray, gray, gray

Gray, gray, gray
  Day after day after day
When a man pinned a rose to his gray lapel
  He was lost to the ranks and condemned to hell
For stepping from line and for getting away
  From gray, gray, GRAY!

Marmalade

Thick cut, thin cut, we all know the drill
From oranges from Africa, more usually
   Seville
Bittersweet like everything the British treasure
   most
Breakfast ISN'T British without marmalade on
   toast!

Suck an Orange

Suck an orange till it's dry
Quench a burning need
But just in case tomorrow's hot
Also plant the seed

Orange Country

Wherever the sun beats long and hard for
    hours in the sky
And people long for evening and a breeze to
    hover by
Wherever the bay and laurel beat the dust and
    drought and grow
There you'll find the orange tree — aglow

The Marigold and the Sun

When the sun is in the sky
When the sun's out so am I
But when the sun is indisposed
Don't expect much — I'll be closed

Sorry, Goldfish

China bred you, China brought you
    To the ornamental pond
Where your gleaming fin gave glimpses
    Of exotic worlds beyond
China bred you, China brought you
    To the common household bowl
Where the ginger tabby waited —
    Thought you lunch and ate you whole

Orangeade—A Recipe For

Grate the rind from oranges—five
   Grate the rind from lemons—two
Squeeze and strain the juice from both
   And this is all there's left to do
Melt one pound (two cups) of sugar
   In four pints of water—cold
Simmer, do not boil, take it off the heat
   Stir in juice and rind and hold
Wait until it's cool
   Chill (of course you would)
Serve with ice and soda
   Sigh, THAT'S GOOD!

Brassy Lass

There once was a lass from Likasi
Who thought herself frightfully classy
Then she broke all the rules
By wearing cheap jewels
And ended up feeling quite brassy

Phinonycteris aurantia, the Bat

Phinonycteris aurantia, the Bat
   Wears a furry orange robe without a hat
And he's found in this regalia
   Round the graves of North Australia
Where you're welcome to pop up and have a chat

Phinonycteris aurantia, the Bat
   Is as orange as an orange—fancy that
So unlike his fellow flyers
   Who steal black as night right by us
You can always see which cemet'ry he's at

Down in the Orangery, Now

Once in the Hothouse orange trees bloomed
   And lovers went down there to kiss
But if you go down to the Orangery now
   There's something you'll probably miss
For though there are orange trees tended and groomed
   And benches for lovers to boot
There's no heady scent, for the flowers and leaves
   Are plastic—and so is the fruit

Whitewash

Ma Hickory's house was in such disrepair
    That birds, bats, and bugs had nested in there
The crevices crumbled, the paint flaked away
    The woodworms, were in and intending to stay
Till Bodgit and Scarper arrived in their van
    "M'z Hickory, ma'am, we will do what we can,"
They lied as they reached for their buckets of lime
    And sploshed in some water and stirred double-time
"We'll soon make it good and so shipshape and white
    You'll hardly believe it's your house by tonight!"
And slap went their brushes, slap slap, round the place
    Just whitewashing over the problems. Disgrace—
For Ma was so pleased with the gleaming white sight
    That she paid them in cash and she danced with delight
Not seeing, not knowing, that their gains were ill-gotten
    And under the whitewash her house was still rotten.

The Lily

They cast her in plaster and alabaster
    And only felt silly
For nothing could capture her likeness of whiteness
    Nothing could capture the lily

Snow

It fell while we were sleeping
I think it fell all night
It fell just like a blanket
And wrapped the world in white
It took away the edges
And leveled high and low
And made the shortest distance
An eternity of snow

The Polar Bear

Look, look, there's a polar bear
Where? Where? I see no bear
There! There! Turned to go
White as ice! On the floe
No! No! There's no bear
Here, there, or anywhere
No bear at all, what is the fuss—
Well, only this: HE'S NOW SEEN US

Be Gone, Jack Frost

Jack Frost is a-creeping out across the lands
With icicles for fingers he's working with both hands
And where he breathes his breathing is icing up the fen
—Be gone, Jack Frost, and never come here again

Clean White Sheets

Clean white sheets, when the washing's done
    Blowing in the breeze, soaking up the sun
Clean white sheets, once the corners meet
    Ironed smooth and flat, smelling fresh and sweet
Clean white sheets, now I'm counting sheep
    There isn't any other place I'd rather fall asleep

The Whiter Tooth Fairy

We've a very fussy fairy who drops in sometimes
    at night
And she leaves us a dollar fifty if the tooth is
    very white
But for yellow ones or gray ones or for filled ones
    or for brown
She will only leave us five cents which is very
    putting down
So there's William and there's Christopher, (my
    brothers) and there's me
And we're brushing in the bathroom, how we're
    brushing, boy, are we
'Cause from now on when we leave our fairy
    gnashers in the night
We are not accepting five cents so we've got to get
    them white!

White Elephants

The good were arranging a fine church bazaar
　　From the hall of the church, (not the trunk of a car)
They all were determined the sale would do well
　　If only, IF ONLY, they'd something to sell.
"I've some white elephants," breathed Mrs. Gray
　　And better than keeping them hidden away
Someone might want them, I can't think for what
　　And we needn't charge much, p'rhaps a dollar the lot"
"And I've a sombrero, I've never yet worn,"
　　Said good Mrs. Brown, "just a teeny bit torn"
"And I've a stuffed owl that once was the craze,"
　　Piped up Mrs. Green. "and a hideous vase"
Then all the good women found something to pledge
　　Something to offer, something to dredge
From the back of a cupboard, an attic, a drawer
　　That they never much liked or would use anymore
Which sold out like hotcakes next day at the sale
　　Making the point of this rather long tale
That what's dross to George may be pure gold to Grace
　　And in the end EVERYTHING does find its place.

Green Behind the Ears

If you are called a greenhorn
   Or green behind the ears
Take no offense (though some is meant
   By those of many years)
For all it says in its mild way
   Is this: Your spring's just sprung
Your life is new and it's quite clear
   That you are very young

Green Fingers

Mrs. McGinty had fingers of green
   It wasn't believed until it was seen
What Mrs. McGinty could grow, I mean
   'Tatoes, tomatoes, cauli and bean
Carrot and broc'li with turnip between
   Geraniums pink and geraniums red
Orchids exotic and none of them dead
   Profusions of fuchsias and roses in tubs
Flowering cherries and flowering shrubs
And all from the having of fingers so green
   And all in an ordin'ry soup tureen

Ten Green Bottles

Ten green bottles hanging on the wall
   If one green bottle should accidentally fall
There'll be nine green bottles hanging from the wall

Nine green bottles hanging on the wall
   If one green bottle should accidentally fall
There'll be eight green bottles hanging from the wall

Eight, seven, six, five, four, three, two…

One green bottle hanging on the wall
   If one green bottle should accidentally fall
There'll be NO green bottles hanging from the wall

Green Cheese

"The moon is made from green cheese"
For centuries people cried
Till Armstrong, Aldrin, and Collins
Discovered they had lied

Green Peace

I'd leave the road on summer days
    Along the path I knew
Beside the clear and babbling stream
    Where Lady's Slippers grew
And find my place inside the wood
    Where insects twinkled gold
And warblers fussed in emerald trees
    Dependable and old
And there I'd sit, alone and still
    And breathe the green like air
Until my old friend, Peace, arrived –
    We always met in there

The Green-eyed Monster

Jealousy's a monster and its eyes are slimy green
    And it has a slimy look upon its face
And once it's up and running, using wicked guile and cunning
    It will nobble any rival in the race

Yes, Jealousy's a monster though it's hardly ever seen
    For it slithers in before we know it's there
But once behind our feelings it will orchestrate our dealings
    Making US the green-eyed monsters—So BEWARE!

Quite Green with It

Ellie was sick, Ellie was ailing
   Her skin was as green as a leaf
A doctor was called, two nurses installed
   Her mother was crying with grief,
"Oh, what is the matter, dear doctor, dear man
   Diagnose it as quick as quick as you can
Has she eaten too much or something that's bad
   Or was it those trifles I know that she had
For though she's no glutton and only gets thinner
   She does like her puddings and does like her dinner…"

Now the doctor was good, as good as you'll get
   As good as a mother could find
But though he was called and nurses installed
   They couldn't read Eleanor's mind
For the matter, in fact, with young Ellie that night
   Was nothing to do with her diet, poor mite,
But simply a terrible vivid green dose
   Of a thing that is caught from being too close
To those who have everything when you have not
   Called Wanting-What-Everyone-Else-Has-Got

The Green Light

If it's red
STOP
If it's yellow
PAUSE
If it's green
GO AHEAD
The world is yours

Greens, Greens, Eat Your Greens

Greens, greens, eat your greens
    Put some on your knife
For greens are full of living things
    Greens are full of life

Greens, greens, eat your greens
    Every time you're fed
Then you'll be full of living things
    A living thing, not dead

Greener Grass

Now, two sheep lived on a luscious hillside
    But they weren't content and they weren't satisfied
They looked through the hedge at the field next door
    And they quite believed what they thought they saw
"Why the grass is greener and the fact of the matter
    Is the sheepdog's finer and the flock is fatter"
So they nibbled through the hedge till they GOT next door
    Where they couldn't believe what they really saw
For the grass wasn't greener and the fact of the matter
    Was the sheepdog was shabby and the flock wasn't fatter
So they looked through the hedge at the field NEXT door
    And they quite believed what they thought they saw
"Why the grass is greener and the fact of the matter
    Is the sheepdog's finer and the flock's much fatter"
So they nibbled through the hedge till they GOT next door
    Where they couldn't believe what they really saw
For the grass wasn't greener and the fact of the matter
    Was the sheepdog was shabby and the flock wasn't fatter
But the two went on going from door to door
    In the hopes they'd find what they thought they saw
"Why the grass there's greener and the flock there's fatter
    And the sheepdog's finer," but the fact of the matter
Is it never was greener in the field next door
    But that's what they wanted—so that's what they saw!

Green Gown

Daffy-down dilly is new come to town
In a yellow petticoat and a green gown

Brown Owl

Brown Owl sits and stares and winks
    And looks as though she wisely thinks
And knows the spirit, essence, sum
    Of all on life's curriculum
Yet I bet we'd prob'ly find
    If we could read the Brown Owl's mind
Of mysteries and hidden meanings
    Sciences and sudden gleanings
Languages and complex words
    She knows no more than other birds
But if I'm wrong and she's the goods
    The Albert Einstein of the woods
It surely comes as no surprise
    'Twas listening that made her wise

The Nut-browns

Almonds, walnuts, hazels, cob
    Chestnuts roasted on the hob
Cashews, filberts, and there's still
    Pine nuts, pecans, and Brazil
Yet how this nut-brown rhyme deceives
    For it's describing autumn leaves

Brownies

Faraway in England, a Brownie isn't sweet
   It isn't made with chocolate, it isn't good to eat
Brownies are hobgoblins, small with lots of hair
   And if you went to England you'd see them everywhere
Putting out the garbage, scrubbing out the sink
   Tidying up the playroom, fast as you can blink
And all they ask for hard work is little gifts of food
   Though don't expect a single scrap of Brownie gratitude…
For here's the catch with Brownies, they cannot stand the thought
   The work they do is known about or bargained for or bought
So, when leaving food for Brownies, if ever comes the day
   You find yourself in England, then do it in this way
Leave it…sort of…lying…accidentally on high shelves
   So the Brownies get the feeling that they found it FOR THEMSELVES.

Brown Paper

Brown paper's thick and brown paper's strong
And brown paper's useful 'cause it lasts so long
And brown paper's best when you've got some string
And you're wrapping up any sort of funny-shaped thing

Brown Bear

My North American Grizzly Bear
    When he's not skulking in his lair
May well be fishing by the lake
    Or searching out a honey cake

My North American Grizzly Bear
    When he's not here, he's always there
Or sharpening up his yellow claws
    Or pushing open cabin doors

My North American Grizzly Bear
    Is not the sort to call, "My dear"
Unless of course it's time for bed
    When he returns to being Ted

Hot Comfort

In all the world, of anything
Of all the drinks most comforting
There's none I'd like to nominate
As warming up hot choc-o-late

Vinegar & Brown Paper

Jack and Jill went up the hill
    To fetch a pail of water
Jack fell down and broke his crown
    And Jill came tumbling after

Then up Jack got and home did trot
    As fast as he could caper
And went to bed and patched his head
    With vinegar and brown paper

Going Brown

I'm not going to pieces and I'm not going to ground
And I'm not going crazy and I'm not going round
And I'm not going to seed and I'm not going to touch
And I'm not going halves and I'm not going Dutch
And I'm not going up and I'm not going down

I'm lying in the sun, going brown

Toffee Nose

Swell, snob, bigwig, nob
Off his lordship goes
Hope he grows a wooden peg
And a toffee nose

Brown Bill and Brown Bess

In fifteen hundred and fifty-four
  Brown Bill was the thing to take to war
A mix of an axe, a spear, and mace
  'Twas most unwieldy about the place
But in eighteen hundred and fifty-two
  Things certainly changed, about time, too
She came with a flint and lock, no less
  The beautiful walnut-stocked Brown Bess!

Gone Puce

When someone you know next goes purple
With rage or imagined abuse
You'd be right to say, "Oh! you've gone flea-colored!"
As the French for a flea is *une puce*

Mauve Monsters

Round the town, when I was young, old ladies went in droves
   Their hair was colored curiously, a sea of different mauves
I hid behind my mother's back while finding ways to peep
   Deciding they were monsters who'd come shopping from the deep
And still a little chilled and thrilled, I wonder to this day
   Why no one thought to tell them we'd have MUCH preferred them gray

Sugared Violets

Perched like tiny butterflies
   Under a clear glass dome
The sweetly scented violets lay
   And thought, no doubt, of home
For captured now and crystallized
   And far from woodland streams
These sweetly sugared violets
   Were topping chocolate creams

A Royal Rage

He was livid, he was purple, he was heliotrope with rage
    He was Emperor and knew it all too well
Yet he wondered how his subjects and his citizens and serfs
    Would know that he was Emperor or tell

"Bring me robes," he said, "of purple and the color of my anger
    For I'm Emperor Celestial on High
And everyone should know it, every citizen and serf
    Every subject passing accidentally by"

So they brought him robes of purple and of heliotrope, magenta
    And they said, "Imperial Highness, you're a wow!"
And immediately his fury and his purple rage subsided
    Now he felt he *looked* an Emperor—and how!

Mulberry Bush

Here we go round the mulberry bush
The mulberry bush, the mulberry bush
Here we go round the mulberry bush
    On a cold and frosty morning

Lavender in Purple Verse

Ah! Lavender, 'tis well you grow
   In clouds of blue, traced with red
To bring us lavender, pure lavender,
   Your own sweet hue.
Wild you sprang at first, on thankless ground
   Then let yourself be tamed.
Field on field, under a beating sun
   And since, how many heated brows and throbbing wrists
Have your cool waters stilled?
   How many cottons, linens, silks
Have your enduring flowers made fragrant and perfumed?
   And what of summers past and childhood paths?
Though you but brushed them lightly
   Are they not all lavender remembered still?

Shrinking Violet

Of all the flowers in the wood
   That ornament the ground
The one that peeps most shyly
   Is the violet — it's found
As if afraid of being crushed
   Ashamed for being small
It seems to half apologize
   For being there at all
And that is why we often say
   Of someone that we love,
"Ah yes, a shrinking violet,"
   When acting as above.

The Foxglove and the Heather

In the highlands, in the heather
   Foxglove raised its head,
"I bring gloves for well-dressed foxes
   You just stay in bed."
In the highlands, Heather answered
Spoke her weathered mind,
   "I bring charms, much-needed fortune
Luck to all mankind."

Lilac Time

Go down to Kew in lilac time, in lilac time, in
   lilac time
Go down to Kew in lilac time (it isn't far from
   London)
And you shall wander hand in hand with love
   in summer's wonderland;
Go down to Kew in lilac time (it isn't far from
   London)